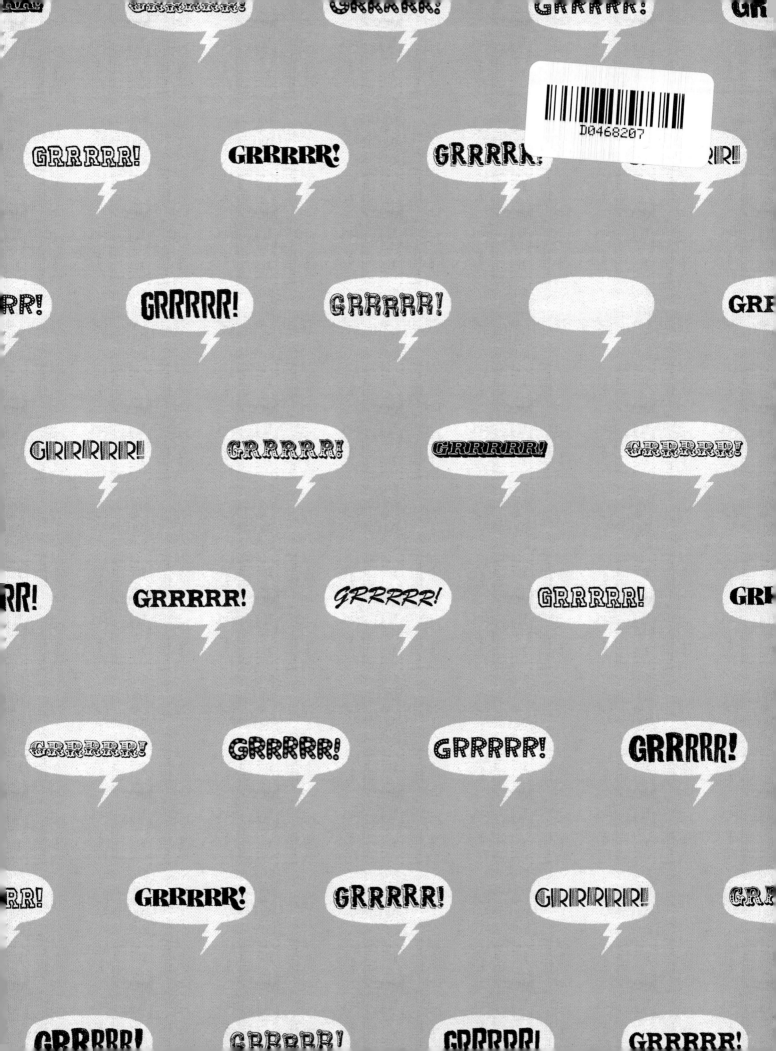

# THE GRIZZLY BEAR WHO LOST HIS GRRRRR!

Written and illustrated by

## Rob Biddulph

**HARPER**

*An Imprint of HarperCollinsPublishers*

# For Ella, Kitty, & Poppy

Library of Congress Control Number: 2015947480

ISBN 978-0-06-236725-9 (trade bdg.)

The artist used a pencil, some paper, a scanner,
Photoshop CS5, a Wacom Tablet, and a Cintiq
6D Art Pen to create the digital illustrations for
this book.
16 17 18 19 20  SCP  10 9 8 7 6 5 4 3 2 1
❖
First U.S. edition, 2016
Originally published in Great Britain by
HarperCollins Children's Books in 2015.

GRIZZLY **BEAR** WHO LOST **HIS**

**R** **R** **R** **R!**

Each year, for as long as the forest has stood,
a contest is held for the bears of the wood.

And the bear who has won for three years in a row
is a grizzly called Fred—he's the star of the show.

A brilliant fish catcher . . .

a fine Hula-Hooper . . .

at scaring the humans he's really quite super. . . .

There's one thing, however, for which he's best known:

When Fred does his loud GRRRRR,
he's out on his own.

He's on his own too,
all day long, while he's training.
There's no time for buddies,
but Fred's not complaining:

Now, this guy is Boris—the new bear in town.
He's entered the contest to win Fred Bear's crown.

He's big and he's strong and he's fast and he's clever.
They say that his GRRRRR is the loudest GRRRRR ever.

But why is he trying to keep out of sight,
so sneaky and quiet in the still of the night?

He's leaving Fred's cave—if you didn't know better,
you'd swear that he had something under that sweater.

The day of the contest, and this could spell trouble:
Poor Fred's woken up with no GRRRRR in his bubble!

What terrible luck! What a shame! What a bore!
Two hours till the contest and

# FRED'S LOST HIS ROAR!

Meanwhile in the treetop
a helpful young owl
looks down through the leaves
at the bear with no growl.

With a hoot and a flutter
he jumps from his perch.
"My name is Eugene.
Can I help with the search?"

Not sure what to do and not sure what to say,
Fred smiles at Eugene and he whispers . . .

"OK."

# So . . .

They look in the greenhouse . . .

they look in the shed . . .

they look through the laundry and under the bed . . .

the top of the wardrobe, inside it, behind it . . .

they turn the place over, but still they can't find it!

Then Eugene calls Hepzibah
—she soon appears.

"I'm here for the hunt
and I've brought volunteers."

An army of helpers all
helping our hero . . .

. . . but how many growls do these helpers find? Zero.

Uh-oh! Now it's time
for the contest to start.
Come along, Fred—
get a move on! Think smart!

"Good luck!" shouts Eugene
as Fred leaves in a hurry.
"We'll all come along to
support you—don't worry!"

Best

# Bear in the Wood

Start

08.59.59

First it's the fish catching—Fred is on fire!
Look at that score getting higher and higher!

Fish catch
Fred 279

Next, at the Hula-Hoop,
Boris is spinning.
With five more than Fred
he is definitely winning!

Hula-Hoop
Boris 017

At scaring the humans it's hard to deny
they're both pretty scary—let's call it a tie!

Scaring the humans
Fred 100

Scaring the humans
Boris 100

And now for the loud GRRRRR—the last round of all.
But who's in the lead? Well, it's too close to call.

First up is Boris. A deep breath, and then . . .

# RRRRRR!

Loud GRRRRR
**Growl-o-meter**

Look at the needle!
It's pointing to

TEN!

Now Fred's in the spotlight. He puffs out his chest.
He opens his mouth and he hopes for the best.

What an extraordinary
state of affairs!
Fred lost his GRRRRR,
but his helpers found theirs!

The sound is so loud that it makes Boris jump—
and look what just fell to the ground with a bump!

"Fred's GRRRRR!" says
Eugene. "It was you all along!
You're a bad, bad bear, Boris,
and cheating is wrong!"

GRRRRR!

"It's true," Boris cries.
"I am guilty. I did it.
I went to Fred's cave,
took his growl
and then hid it.

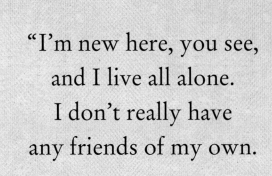

"I'm new here, you see,
and I live all alone.
I don't really have
any friends of my own.

"I hoped that if people
thought I was a winner,
then maybe, sometimes,
they might come 'round
for dinner."

Fred looks at Boris and what does he see?
A bear who is not all that different from he.

A bear
who is
lonely.

A bear
who is sad.

A bear who
is, maybe,
not totally . . .
bad.

"I think we're both winners," says Fred, "and what's more,
I'd like to be friends," and he holds out a paw.

"R-really?" says Boris, who gets to his feet
and gives Fred a bear hug. Oh, isn't that sweet.

They'll always remember how this story ends:
That Fred lost his GRRRRR . . .

but discovered his friends!

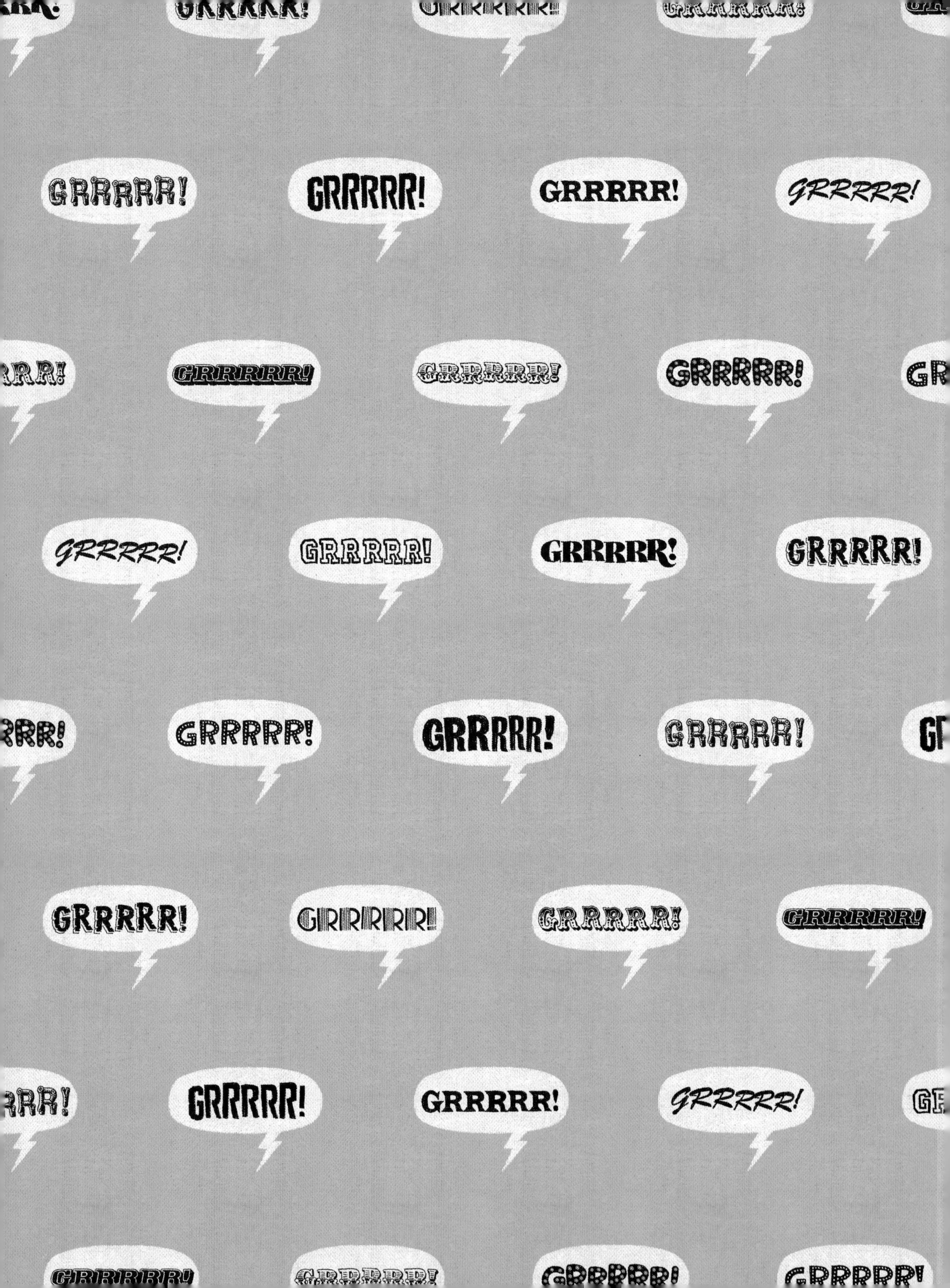